# Kitty
# Runs up a Tree

### Story by Annette Smith
### Illustrations by Ben Spiby

Rigby®

A Harcourt Achieve Imprint

www.Rigby.com
1-800-531-5015

Kitty Cat went
into the garden.
She hid in the flowers.

"Fat Cat is not here,"
she said.
"I am going to eat
his food."

"I like Fat Cat's food,"
said naughty Kitty Cat.

Fat Cat came
into the garden.

"Kitty Cat," he said,
"you are eating my food.
 Go away!"

 Kitty Cat looked up.
"I like your food,"
 said Kitty Cat.

"**Go away!**" said Fat Cat.

9

Kitty Cat ran away.

She ran up a little tree.

She looked down at Fat Cat.

"**You** cannot come up here,"
she said.

"I'm coming to get you,"
said Fat Cat.

Kitty Cat ran
way up the tree.

Fat Cat ran after Kitty Cat.

Fat Cat got
on to a little branch.
The little branch went
down

. . . down

. . . down!


Fat Cat fell off.

"Good," said Kitty Cat.